THE EGYPTIAN WORLD

- BAST -

- NUT -

- RA'S SUN BOAT -

- ANUBIS -

Brownstone's Mythical Collection: Marcy and the Riddle of the Sphinx © Flying Eye Books 2017.
This paperback edition published in 2019. First published in 2017 by Flying Eye Books,
an imprint of Nobrow Ltd. 27 Westgate Street, London E8 3RL.

Text and illustrations © Joe Todd-Stanton 2017.

Joe Todd-Stanton has asserted his right under the Copyright, Designs and
Patents Act, 1988, to be identified as the Author and Illustrator of this Work.

1 3 5 7 9 10 8 6 4 2

Published in the US by Nobrow (US) Inc.

Printed in Poland on FSC® certified paper.

ISBN: 978-1-911171-82-9

Order from www.flyingeyebooks.com

-JOE TODD-STANTON-

BROWNSTONE'S MYTHICAL COLLECTION

MARCY
AND THE
RIDDLE
OF THE
SPHINX

FLYING EYE BOOKS
London - New York

Until one day, he met another adventurer.

Together they moved to a small town and Marcy was born soon after.

Every evening, Marcy loved to listen to the tales of her father's adventures. Though she never quite believed him... After all, he was very old and far too portly.

But at night, everything changed. The creatures from her father's amazing tales turned into terrifying monsters in the shadows. Marcy felt utterly lost and alone in the dark. All she could do was close her eyes tight and wait for sunrise.

One day Arthur decided it was time for Marcy's first adventure. He knew that Marcy doubted his stories, so he took her deep into the forest to find an old friend.

As the day wore on, Marcy started to worry that they wouldn't find their way back in the dark.

Arthur pointed up to the sky and told her that the North Star would always guide them home, no matter how dark it was.

Finally, they reached the entrance of a cave and Marcy froze in fear.
Evil-looking shadows climbed the walls and she refused to go any further.

Hurt that Marcy didn't trust him, and hoping she might follow him, Arthur ventured into the cave alone.

Arthur had wanted to show Marcy the most incredible sight.
But she didn't appear and Arthur had to turn back.

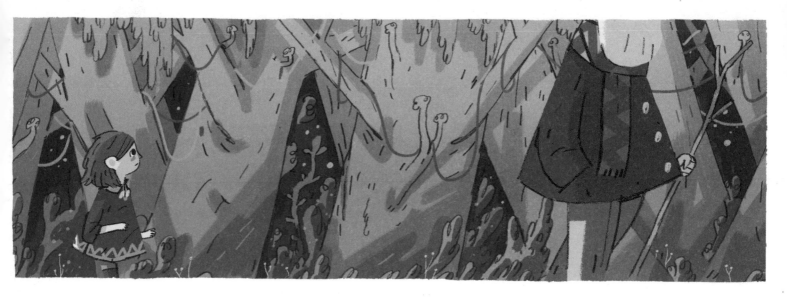

On the walk home, Arthur was very quiet and Marcy was sure he was disappointed in her.

If she couldn't go into a stupid dark cave, then maybe she wasn't an adventurer at all. Maybe she wasn't even a real Brownstone.

The next day Marcy found a note from her father. Her mother said it was nothing to worry about, but Marcy didn't feel happy at all.

A whole week went by and Marcy was so worried that she snuck into her father's study.

Hidden under the piles of papers and old artefacts, Marcy found Arthur's journal.

It showed that her father must have gone to Egypt to find an old book trapped in the belly of the Sphinx. Oh no! Her father had trouble just bending over when he dropped his glasses. Marcy would have to help him ... somehow.

Just then she noticed the magical feathers of Wind Weaver tucked into the brim of her father's old hat.

Arthur had told her that carrying a feather from this mighty bird would grant someone help in a time of need. Marcy smiled and put it on.

Feeling a little braver already, Marcy climbed out of the study window where Wind Weaver was waiting for her!

She felt her chest tighten as they swooped into the air
and began the long journey towards Egypt...

...and the Sphinx.

Marcy landed at the feet of a strange creature sitting on a massive throne.

I am Thoth, god of knowledge and the moon. I know who you are, little girl.

Your father was foolish enough to enter the Sphinx in the hope of getting my book. It seems he wanted to help you with your fear of the dark. You see, whoever possesses my book will understand all the mysteries of the world.

Marcy was far too scared to enter the dark tomb and begged Thoth to release her father.

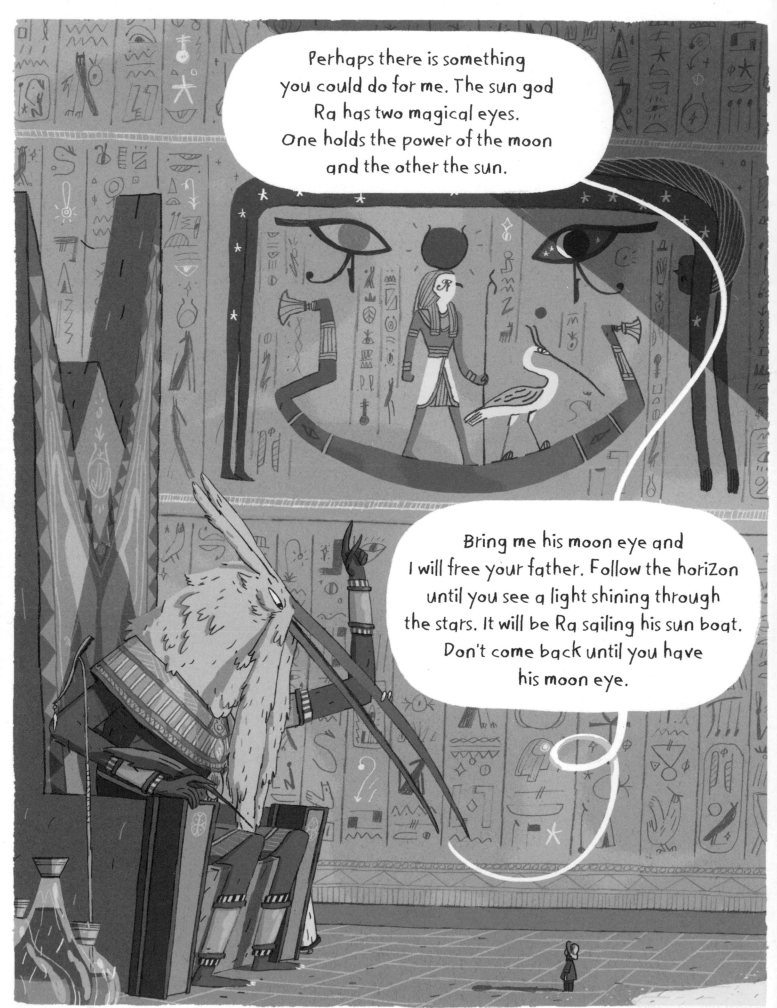

Perhaps there is something you could do for me. The sun god Ra has two magical eyes. One holds the power of the moon and the other the sun.

Bring me his moon eye and I will free your father. Follow the horizon until you see a light shining through the stars. It will be Ra sailing his sun boat. Don't come back until you have his moon eye.

With Thoth's words ringing in her ears, Marcy wandered through the desert towards the horizon. Suddenly, she saw what looked like a shooting star.

It was getting bigger...

...and bigger.

Marcy had to act quickly.

At the ship's helm, Marcy could see the god Ra. But first she would have to remain unnoticed by the boat's crew of gods...

...Anubis, god of the afterlife...

...Isis, goddess of nature and magic...

...and Bast, goddess of cats.

With Ra in sight, Marcy came up with a plan to get his eye.

But as she readied herself for the jump, she realised she couldn't steal someone else's eye! For all she knew, Ra could be a very nice god.

She bravely climbed down the rigging and walked slowly up behind him. She was very small so she had to clear her throat as she gave a big tug on his cape.

Ra was intrigued by the little human who had found her way
on to his sun boat. He listened to her story before speaking.

Thank you for your honesty.
Thoth is always plotting
to steal my moon eye.

"If Thoth were ever to get hold of it, he would become unspeakably powerful and plunge the whole world into evil.

As a reward for your service, I will help you free your father."

"My boat will take us to the Sphinx. The goddess of the night sky,
Nut, will show us the way by shining a path in the stars," said Ra.

As Ra's ship reached the Sphinx, an anchor dropped down.
Just before Marcy went to climb down, Ra knelt before her.

Here, take my sun eye.
Its light will guide you and cut
through the darkest shadows.
Good luck!

Marcy was filled with excitement.
Maybe she was a real Brownstone after all?

The Sphinx loomed up ahead.
As she approached it spoke its riddle.

I am bright when it's dark,
and dark when it's bright.
I am the shepherd of the night.
Who am I?

Marcy had never heard of a night shepherd before ... what could it possibly mean?
She thought and she thought some more but she couldn't think of the answer.

And then she had a sudden idea. What was only at its brightest
in the dark ... the stars! And shepherds guide things... Of course!

The North Star!

The Sphinx's mouth opened to reveal a set of steps.
They led down into a deep, dark cave.

Marcy trembled with fear, but she knew
this was the only way to save her father…

As she descended into the belly of the Sphinx, it got darker...

...and darker.

When Marcy finally found Arthur, he was too busy with the huge snake to hear her shouts. She didn't have time to think. She had to do something!

With the eye of Ra lighting her way, she vaulted straight into the snake's mouth!

In that moment, Arthur realised the book would not help Marcy. She had already overcome her fear. He dropped it and they escaped together.

Outside the Sphinx, a shadowy figure was waiting for them and an evil voice boomed...

Marcy tried to tell Thoth it was the wrong eye but it was too late.

As he took the eye, there was a flash of white,

a crack of thunder and then silence...

All that was left of Thoth was a tiny bird and Ra's magic eye.

Ra appeared and picked up his eye,
placing the tiny bird on his shoulder.

Together they all climbed up on to
Ra's sun boat and prepared for home.

Nut guided the sun boat by shining
the North Star as brightly as she could.

When they were finally home, Marcy couldn't wait to tell her parents
every single detail about her adventure in the land of Egypt.

And when it was time for Marcy to go to sleep,
for the first time, she didn't feel scared at all.

THE EGYPTIAN WORLD

SCARAB

NUT

RA'S SUN BOAT

UNKNOWN

If you enjoyed this book, read more from the Brownstone family's incredible adventures in:

Brownstone's Mythical Collection: Arthur and the Golden Rope
Paperback ISBN: 978-1-911171-69-0
Hardback ISBN: 978-1-911171-03-4

When avid adventurer Arthur is accused of leading a monstrous wolf into his town and it destroys their great fire, it falls on him to travel to the Viking gods, capture the beast and save his home from freezing over. He's been on so many adventures before, how much harder could this one be?

www.flyingeyebooks.com